Self Defender

by Jane West
illustrated by Lee Wildish

Librarian Reviewer
Marci Peschke
Librarian, Dallas Independent School District
MA Education Reading Specialist, Stephen F. Austin State University
Learning Resources Endorsement, Texas Women's University

Reading Consultant
Sherry Klehr
Elementary/Middle School Educator, Edina Public Schools, MN
MA in Education, University of Minnesota

STONE ARCH BOOKS
Minneapolis   San Diego

First published in the United States in 2008
by Stone Arch Books
151 Good Counsel Drive, P.O. Box 669
Mankato, Minnesota 56002
www.stonearchbooks.com

Originally published in Great Britain in 2006
by Badger Publishing Ltd

Original work copyright © 2006 Badger Publishing Ltd
Text copyright © 2006 Jane West

The right of Jane West to be identified as the author
of this work has been asserted by her in accordance
with the Copyright, Designs and Patent Act 1988.

Library of Congress Cataloging-in-Publication Data
West, Jane, 1959–
    [Striking Out]
    Self Defender / by Jane West; illustrated by Lee Wildish.
    p. cm. — (Keystone Books)
    ISBN 978-1-4342-0477-6 (library binding)
    ISBN 978-1-4342-0527-8 (paperback)
    [1. Bullies—Fiction. 2. Self-defense—Fiction.] I. Wildish, Lee, ill.
II. Title.
PZ7.W5178Se 2008
[Fic]—dc22   2007028515

1 2 3 4 5 6 13 12 11 10 09 08

Printed in the United States of America

Table of Contents

CHAPTER 1

New School

In September, Tess was going to a new school. Again.

Tess was used to her dad changing jobs. He had been doing it her whole life. When her dad got a new job, Tess got a new house, new friends, and a new school.

Tess had been to five schools. Everyone said it would be easier the next time, but it never was.

The first day of the year at Tess's new school wasn't too bad. Two girls had volunteered to show her around.

"Hi! I'm Mandy," said the one with glasses.

"And I'm Val," said the one with the long, dark hair.

They smiled at her and Tess began to relax. "I'm Tess," she said shyly.

CHAPTER 2

Ellie Jones

The new school was okay, but on Wednesday, everything started to go wrong.

Tess met Val and Mandy for lunch. She got her tray and chose a pizza and salad with a milkshake, and sat down at one of the long tables.

"That's my seat, worm," said a mean voice. A tall girl with blond hair was staring down at Tess.

"I'm sorry," said Tess quietly. "I didn't know."

"Well, now you do," said the girl. "Move it or lose it."

Tess got up quickly, but not before the girl spilled Tess's milkshake all over her pizza.

"Oops!" said the girl. "Ugh! Looks like puke. The worm is eating puke!" The other girls laughed.

Tess walked away. There were tears in her eyes. She sat down at the back of the room and stared at her soggy lunch.

Val and Mandy walked over and sat down with her.

"That was Ellie Jones," said Val. "She's the meanest girl in school."

"She really is," agreed Mandy. "I've even seen her fight boys!"

"Everything all right here?" asked a teacher, looking at the three girls.

"Yes," said Tess quietly. "It's fine."

CHAPTER 3

Or Else

Tess was walking home from school with Val.

A voice said, "Oh look! It's the worm." Ellie Jones pushed her large face into Tess's and spit at her.

Angry and upset, Tess yelled, "What did you do that for?"

"Because I don't like you, worm," Ellie said. "What are you looking at?" she shouted at Val.

"Nothing," mumbled Val.

"Well, get lost!" Ellie said.

Val ran away. Then Tess was alone with Ellie Jones. Ellie lowered her voice as she pushed Tess up against a wall.

"Don't mess with me," Ellie growled, "or you'll be sorry. I want five dollars by tomorrow. Don't tell anyone, or else."

She pushed Tess to the ground. Tess's bag fell into the street.

Then Ellie walked away, laughing.

CHAPTER 4

Coward

Tess cried the whole way home.

Her mom knew that something was wrong. "What happened?" she asked.

Tess told her the whole story.

"She sounds awful, honey," said her mom. "You have to stand up to bullies. They're just cowards. They need to hurt other people to feel better about themselves. I want you to tell your teacher tomorrow."

"But Ellie said I'd be sorry if I did!" Tess cried.

"Bullies can only hurt people if nobody says anything. You have to tell your teacher," said her mom gently.

CHAPTER 5

Telling Lies

The next day, Tess told her teacher, Mrs. Price, about Ellie.

Mrs. Price said, "I'll handle this."

Right before lunch, Tess was called into the principal's office. Ellie was there, too. She was crying.

"Tell me exactly what's been going on," said the principal, Mr. Hill.

Ellie said she'd stopped to talk to Tess on the way home from school.

Then Ellie said that Tess's bag had fallen into the street by mistake.

"No!" Tess yelled. "She pushed me on purpose!"

"Well, it's your word against hers," Mr. Hill said.

He looked at Ellie and said, "I'm sure Ellie would like to apologize for what happened."

"Sorry!" Ellie said, sniffling.

Ellie's tears stopped as soon they left the office. "You're the one who'll be sorry," she whispered angrily. "You'll be sorry you ever showed your ugly face in this school. And it'll be a lot uglier by the time I'm done with you. See you after school, worm."

Shakily, Tess walked to the cafeteria. Her cell phone beeped. There was a text message. It read: **C U after school.** There was no name, but Tess knew who it was from.

Tess ran to the girls' bathroom. She hid there until lunch was over. She ran home as soon as the bell rang after school.

Over and over, the same question went through her head.

"What am I going to do?"

CHAPTER 6

Self-Defense

When Tess got home, her mom asked, "Did that girl bother you again?"

"No," muttered Tess.

Her mom sighed. "Well, why don't you check the movie listings. We could go see a movie to cheer you up."

Tess paged through the local paper looking for the movie listings. A small advertisement caught her eye.

```
 lass    Self-Defense Class
ucated,   for Beginners
a new    Discover a new you!
age.     6:30 p.m. on Tuesday
         Hamble City Center

         Learn French
```

"That's it!" said Tess excitedly.
"That's just what I need!"

Tess asked her mom if it was okay
for her to go.

"I think it is a great idea," said
Tess's mom.

When Tess got to the class, she saw
that the room was full of people in
white outfits. There was a small group
of people like Tess, who were wearing
T-shirts and sweats.

"Welcome!" said a young woman. "My name is Jen. I'm going to teach you how to defend yourselves."

Jen was slim and not much taller than Tess.

"I'll show you that size doesn't matter," Jen went on.

A huge, hulking man with tattoos on his muscles stood next to her.

"Neil is going to try to throw me," said Jen.

Neil lunged at Jen, but she got out of the way.

Then she grabbed the front of his shirt and threw him over her shoulder. The huge man landed on the floor with a thud.

"Wow!" said Tess. "That was so cool!"

"Thanks," said Jen. "You'll be able to do that soon!"

Tess spent the next hour learning some simple self-defense moves. She went home hot, sweaty and tired, but happy.

"Just you wait, Ellie Jones," she said to herself. "Just you wait!"

CHAPTER 7

Waiting

Tess went to self-defense classes for the next four weeks.

She loved the class. She loved it so much that her mom let her join a judo class too.

Tess felt pretty cool in her judo outfit, although it was annoying that she had to keep her nails short.

Tess learned how to fall without hurting herself.

She also learned how to throw people off balance, even if they were heavier and taller than she was.

Jen had been right about that. Size didn't matter when you knew judo.

At school, Tess stayed out of Ellie's way. Sometimes she saw Ellie watching her from a distance.

The text messages kept coming. Tess didn't delete them. She knew the day was coming when Ellie would attack her again. This time, Tess would be ready. And she'd have proof that Ellie was a bully.

One day, Tess, Val, and Mandy were sitting in their classroom when Tess got another text message from Ellie. It said: **2nite, worm. No 1 will help u.**

Mandy and Val looked scared. Tess said, "Ellie Jones is a bully, but she doesn't scare me."

Mandy and Val looked at her in shock. Tess just smiled.

CHAPTER 8

Sweet Revenge!

At lunch that day, Tess was standing in line when Ellie Jones walked up.

"I'm going to get you tonight," Ellie growled.

"Do I look worried?" said Tess in a bored voice.

"Move, worm!" shouted Ellie. She tried to push Tess.

In a flash, Tess grabbed the arm that was pushing her.

Tess spun like she'd been taught in judo, and pulled hard. Ellie flew onto the ground.

Ellie skidded on the floor and landed face first in a pizza. Then her carton of milk exploded and spilled all over her head.

Mandy and Val started giggling and Tess laughed out loud.

Soon, the whole lunchroom was shrieking with laughter. Ellie had pizza sauce dripping down her nose.

"You ruined my lunch, pizza face!" said Tess with a laugh.

"Miss Jones!" said the lunchtime supervisor. "There will be no bullying in my lunchroom. Go to the principal's office!"

Ellie's face was burning with shame. Milk dripped down her hair and onto her pizza-covered face, leaving a slimy trail behind her.

"That was amazing!" shouted Val.

"I can teach you, if you want," said Tess, smiling. "But I don't think Ellie Jones will be bullying anyone ever again . . . not if she knows what's good for her!"

About the Author

Jane West has been writing all her life. She worked in advertising and as a teacher before she became a full-time writer in 2001. Her favorite job/hobby/thing-in-the-whole-world is writing stories for children. Jane lives in Cornwall with her husband and Jack Russell puppy named Pip, who is her inspiration. She says, "Writing stories is the best job in the world, and the best feeling is when someone says they like your story."

🌸 Glossary

advertisement (ad-ver-TIZE-muhnt)—a public notice that calls attention to something, like a product or an event

coward (KOW-urd)—someone who is scared

defense (dih-FENSS)—to protect something

judo (JOO-doh)—a sport in which two people fight each other using quick, controlled movements, each trying to throw the other to the ground

purpose (PUR-puhss)—if you do something on purpose, you mean to do it

revenge (ri-VENJ)—action that you take to pay someone back for harm that the person has done to you or to someone you care about

shyly (SHYE-lee)—if you say something shyly, you are nervous and quiet as you say it

soggy (SOG-ee)—very wet, soaked

supervisor (SOO-pur-vye-zur)—someone who watches over something

volunteered (vol-uhn-TEERD)—offered to do a job

Discussion Questions

1. Tess takes self-defense classes so that she can protect herself from a bully. What are some other reasons to take self-defense classes? Talk about them.

2. What are some good ways to stop a bully? What should you do if someone is bullying you?

3. Tess is at a new school for the fifth time. How should you treat a new kid at school? What are some ways to help them feel more comfortable?

# Writing Prompts

1. Have you ever known a bully? How did you handle the situation? Write about it.

2. Sometimes it can be interesting to think about a story from another person's point of view. Try writing chapter 8 from Ellie's point of view. What does she think about? How does she experience what happens? Write it down.

3. In this book, Tess is lucky to make friends with two girls on her first day of school. Have you ever been in a situation where you needed to make new friends? What did you do? Write about it.

Also by Jane West

Mystery in Mexico

Sam loves exploring the Mexican jungle with her dad. One hot, sleepy day, Sam decides to do a little exploring on her own. But she quickly finds herself in terrible danger!

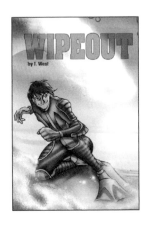

Wipeout

Jake doesn't think there's anything good about the ocean until he meets Sully. Sully teaches Jake some cool bodyboarding tricks. Soon, Jake is good enough to enter a competition. But what kind of friend is Sully if he doesn't want Jake to be in the contest?

The Star Key
by Melanie Joyce

On Tyler's thirteenth birthday she is given a strange note, written by her long-dead grandmother. Tyler learns that she has a special, secret destiny. Only she can save the world from terrible danger!

The Messenger Bag
by Jillian Powell

Stacey is sick of her unstylish handbag. One day, Stacey finds a beautiful old Kelly bag. She takes it everywhere. The bag hides a secret that's meant only for Stacey.

🌸 Internet Sites

Do you want to know more about subjects related to this book? Or are you interested in learning about other topics? Then check out FactHound, a fun, easy way to find Internet sites.

Our investigative staff has already sniffed out great sites for you!

Here's how to use FactHound:

1. Visit *www.facthound.com*

2. Select your grade level.

3. To learn more about subjects related to this book, type in the book's ISBN number: **9781434204776**.

4. Click the **Fetch It** button.

FactHound will fetch the best Internet sites for you!